# Double Puppy Trouble

## DANICA McKELLAR

illustrated by **Josée Masse**

Crown Books for Young Readers

New York

Hello there, my friend! Are you ready to meet
Someone spunky, ambitious, and playfully sweet?
She craved big adventures, to learn and to grow.
Here she is: the unstoppable Miss Moxie Jo!

She liked to climb trees and compete in most sports,
Give cuddles, solve puzzles, play games of all sorts.

It's clear that she had a bright future in store.
The problem with Moxie? She had to have MORE.

MORE game-winning goals, MORE cookies and books.

MORE bracelets and trinkets. (And everyone looks!)

MORE height on the tree and MORE time on the swing.

MORE A's on her tests—but here was the thing:

MATH EXAM
Name Moxie

$1 \times 2 = 2$    $32 \times 2 = 64$
$2 \times 2 = 4$    $64 \times 2 = 128$
$4 \times 2 = 8$    $128 \times 2 = 256$
$8 \times 2 = 16$    $256 \times 2 = 512$
$16 \times 2 = 32$    $512 \times 2 = 1024$

Congratulations!

HISTORY
Name Moxie

What is important about 1776?
Was the year our Founding Fathers
...laration of Independence...

If she didn't have the MOST dolls and MOST A's,
The tallest block towers and game-winning plays,
Or if Clark, her young brother, broke one of her toys,
She'd stomp and she'd cry and she'd make SO MUCH NOISE!

"Stop, Moxie Jo!" said her mom with a shout.
"Nobody's perfect, but things will work out!
Now I have to help Dad, so please *don't* make this hard.
If you need us, we'll be at the back of the yard."

Some days she felt happy. And others? So sad!
Some days she felt giddy. And others? So mad!

Her feelings confused her . . .

Through and through. . . .

Instead of ONE girl . . .

Perhaps she was TWO . . . ?

"Whatever," she huffed as she walked out the door.
"If there's TWO of me, all the reason for MORE.

"And I want more! More, more, MORE!"

Then what did she see? Gee, look what she found:
An odd little stick there, just stuck in the ground.
Two branches came out and then split into TWO.

She wondered, "Now what does *this* big button do?"

"I did that myself? . . . Could it really be . . .
That I can make TWINS of whatever I see?"

Moxie doubled some bubbles, toy trucks, and a shoe.
She doubled a cute little ladybug, too!

But then when she pointed the wand at a flower,
She happened upon an incredible power:
She held IN that button and didn't let go,
And doubles kept doubling and doubling—WHOA!

Every five seconds, they doubled again!
In just twenty seconds, she had more than ten!
First 1 and then 2, and then 4, and then 8.
Now 16 and 32.

This is SO GREAT!

She loved her new power: the power of MORE.
MORE toys and MORE books, MORE than ever before!

Sixty-four cookies and puzzles and cars,
One hundred and twenty-eight bracelets with stars.

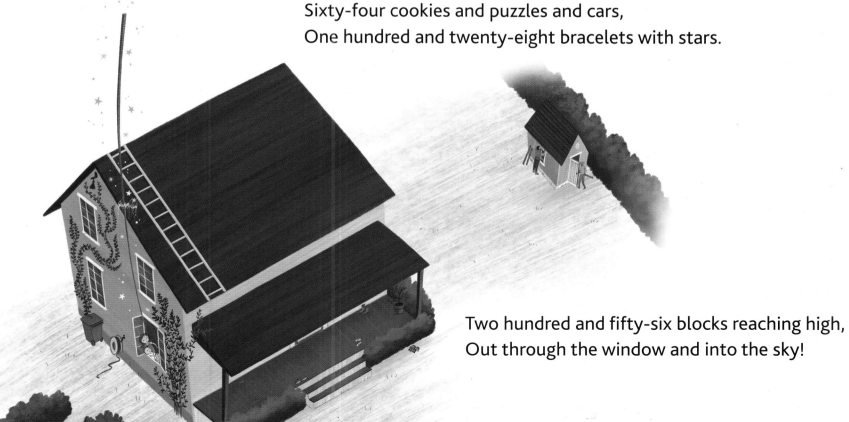

Two hundred and fifty-six blocks reaching high,
Out through the window and into the sky!

And then Moxie stopped—she stopped dead in her tracks.
"I know what to do: make a double of MAX!"
She felt super smart! "No more sharing to do.
Two puppies means there's one for me *and* for you."

First 2, and then 4? And then there were 8!
"I'm not pressing the button! What's happening? Wait!"
The button was STUCK?! Well, this could be troubling. . . .

Those cute little puppies kept doubling and DOUBLING!

Then sixteen sweet puppies, and next? Thirty-two!
Miss Moxie's jaw dropped, and her little eyes grew.
The puppies were doubling now, faster and faster!
It seemed she was in for a major disaster. . . .

They ATE all the cookies and CRASHED all the cars,
Then CHEWED up the bracelets with sparkly blue stars.
They TORE up the books, and they BROKE all the toys.
Their cute little barking made SOOOOOO MUCH NOISE!

Now sixty-four puppies each wanted a hug.
One hundred and twenty-eight nibbled the rug.
The number of pups exponentially grew:
They each multiplied times a factor of 2!

Two hundred and fifty-six scampered around,
Chasing each other and sniffing the ground.
Five hundred and twelve? There's not enough space!
So some of the puppies dashed out of that place,
Straight out of the house and then into the mud.
They turned on the hose and created a flood!

One thousand and twenty-four! Puppies galore!
"But what if this stick *doesn't stop* making MORE?
One minute from now—if this pace keeps up?
That's OVER A MILLION of our little pup!"

2
4
8 16 32 64

128 512 1,024 . . .
256

"Wait, look at the house! What's happening there?"
She ran back inside to find pups EVERYWHERE!

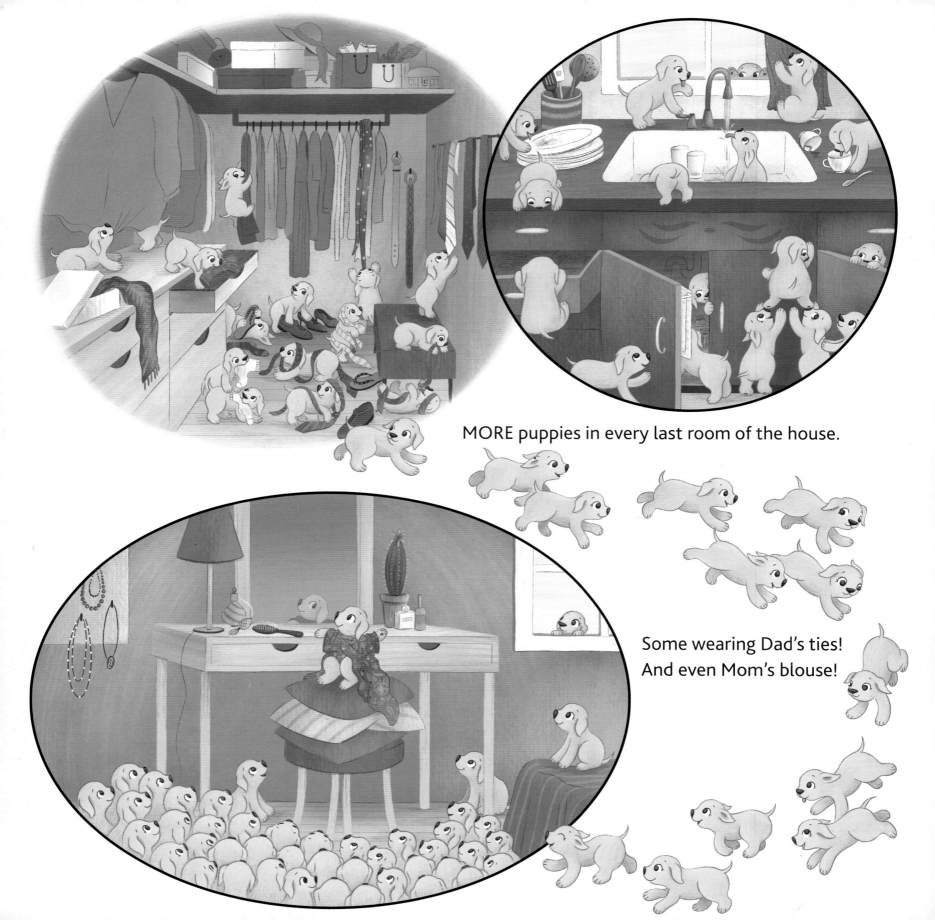

MORE puppies in every last room of the house.

Some wearing Dad's ties!
And even Mom's blouse!

MORE sliding down banisters, climbing the walls,
Or riding on roller skates, cruising the halls.

Some pups on the couch and some taking a bath.

Other pups with a book, perhaps doing some math?

Their sweet muddy paws were all over their stuff. I mean, they were cute, but enough is enough!

Her brother, young Clark, always got in her way.
But something was changing for Moxie that day. . . .

She *noticed* her brother like never before:
With a fire in his eyes and a mop on the floor,
Clark was ready to help her—and with any chore!
Her heart filled with more . . . and more . . . and MORE. . . .

Remember how Clark often broke Moxie's things?
Like lamps and her dolls and her airplane's red wings?

He tripped on a pup and—oops!—stumbled and fell!
Clark broke that big stick, and then *that broke the spell*!

POP!

Woo-hoo!

Moxie was suddenly grateful for LESS.
Now all that was left was to clean up the mess. . . .

When their parents walked in, they knew something was wrong
But were happy to see how their kids got along.

That sister and brother had learned some *new* powers.
When working together, they built TALLER towers,
Baked even MORE cookies . . . got parents to bend . . .

Like adopting a puppy so Max had a friend.

Did Moxie Jo ever still wish she had MORE?
Did she wish she had every toy in the store?
Did she ever get really mad at her brother?
Have plenty of cookies but still want another?

The answer is YES . . . but not quite as often.
Little Miss Moxie had learned how to soften.
She knew the best feelings don't come from more stuff. . . .
It turns out that Moxie had MORE than enough.

# A Whole Lotta Lemons!

What if you wanted to pick 1 lemon on the first day of the month, 2 lemons the next day, 4 lemons the following day, 8 lemons the day after that, and you kept going, doubling the number of lemons each day? Could you keep it up all month long?

| | |
|---|---|
| August 1st: | 🍋 |
| August 2nd: | 🍋🍋 |
| August 3rd: | 🍋🍋🍋🍋 |
| August 4th: | 🍋🍋🍋🍋🍋🍋🍋🍋 |
| August 5th: | 🍋🍋🍋🍋🍋🍋🍋🍋🍋🍋🍋🍋🍋🍋🍋🍋 |

If you started August 1st and doubled the number every day, then at the end of the first week, on August 7th, you'd pick 64 lemons. Not too bad, but that's a REALLY full shopping bag of lemons. Have a grown-up help you carry it, or split it into more than one bag!

But if that seems like a lot, at the end of the second week, on August 14th, you'd have to pick 8,192 lemons—holy cow! That's almost enough lemons to fill up your car!

At the end of week 3, on August 21st, you'd have to pick 1,048,576 lemons—that's over a million lemons! What?! Yes, it's a huge number. It's enough lemons to fill up a house!

And on the 31st day of August, the amount of lemons you'd pick would be an unbelievable 1,073,741,824 lemons! Yep, that's over a *billion* lemons. That's enough lemons to fill a 30-story building!

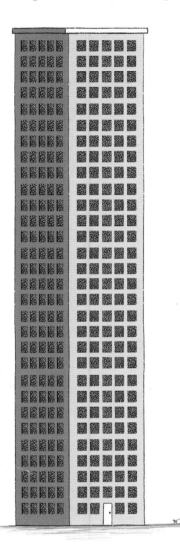

My goodness, all we did was *double the number of lemons* every day. Wow, doubling numbers sure is powerful—those numbers get really big, really quickly. Exponential growth truly is amazing. . . .

## AUGUST

| SUNDAY | MONDAY | TUESDAY | WEDNESDAY | THURSDAY | FRIDAY | SATURDAY |
|---|---|---|---|---|---|---|
| 1<br>1 | 2<br>2 | 3<br>4 | 4<br>8 | 5<br>16 | 6<br>32 | 7<br>64 |
| 8<br>128 | 9<br>256 | 10<br>512 | 11<br>1,024 | 12<br>2,048 | 13<br>4,096 | 14<br>8,192 |
| 15<br>16,384 | 16<br>32,768 | 17<br>65,536 | 18<br>131,072 | 19<br>262,144 | 20<br>524,288 | 21<br>1,048,576 |
| 22<br>2,097,152 | 23<br>4,194,304 | 24<br>8,388,608 | 25<br>16,777,216 | 26<br>33,554,432 | 27<br>67,108,864 | 28<br>134,217,728 |
| 29<br>268,435,456 | 30<br>536,870,912 | 31<br>1,073,741,824 | | | | |

Check out **DoublePuppyTrouble.com** for the details of all the calculations on these pages (using exponents!), where you'll also find ideas on how to get the most from this book—and even a healthy lemonade recipe, too!